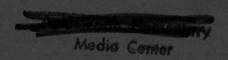

FABLES

FABLES

*Written and
Illustrated
by*
ARNOLD LOBEL

HARPER & ROW, PUBLISHERS

Fables
Copyright © 1980 by Arnold Lobel
Printed in the U.S.A. All rights reserved.
First Edition

Library of Congress Cataloging in Publication Data
Lobel, Arnold.
Fables.

SUMMARY: Twenty original fables about an array of
animal characters from crocodile to ostrich.
1. Fables, American.   2. Children's stories, American.
[1. Animals—Fiction.   2. Fables]   I. Title.
PZ8.2.L6Fab   [Fic]   79-2004
ISBN 0-06-023973-5
ISBN 0-06-023974-3 lib. bdg.

THE FABLES

FABLES

THE CROCODILE IN THE BEDROOM

A Crocodile became increasingly fond of the wallpaper in his bedroom. He stared at it for hours and hours.

"Just look at all those neat and tidy rows of flowers and leaves," said the Crocodile. "They are like soldiers. There is not a single one that is out of place."

"My dear," said the Crocodile's wife, "you are spending too much time in bed. Come out into my garden where the air is fresh and the sun is bright and warm."

"Well, if you insist, for just a few minutes," said the Crocodile. He put on a pair of dark glasses to protect his eyes from the glare and went outside.

Mrs. Crocodile was proud of her garden.

"Look at the hollyhocks and the marigolds," she said. "Smell the roses and the lilies of the valley."

"Great heavens!" cried the Crocodile. "The flowers and leaves in this garden are growing in a terrible tangle! They are all scattered! They are messy and entwined!"

The Crocodile rushed back to his bedroom in a state of great distress. He was at once comforted by the sight of his wallpaper.

"Ah," said the Crocodile. "Here is a garden that is ever so much better. How happy and secure these flowers make me feel!"

After that the Crocodile seldom left his bed. He lay there, smiling at the walls. He turned a very pale and sickly shade of green.

Without a doubt, there is such a thing as too much order.

THE DUCKS AND THE FOX

Two Duck sisters were waddling down the road to the pond for their morning swim.

"This is a good road," said the first sister, "but I think, just for a change, we should find another route. There are many other roads that lead to the pond."

"No," said the second sister, "I do not agree. I really do not want to try a new way. This road makes me feel comfortable. I am accustomed to it."

One morning the Ducks met a Fox sitting on a fence along the road.

"Good morning, ladies," said the Fox. "On your way to the pond, I suppose?"

"Oh, yes," said the sisters, "we come along here every day."

"Interesting," said the Fox with a toothy smile.

When the sun came up the next morning, the first sister said, "We are sure to meet that Fox again if we go our usual way. I did not like his looks. Today is the day that we must find another road!"

"You are being just plain silly," said the second sister. "That Fox smiled at us. He seemed most gentlemanly."

The two Ducks waddled down the same road to the pond. There was the Fox, sitting on the fence. This time he carried a sack.

"Lovely ladies," said the Fox, "I was expecting you. I am glad that you have not disappointed me."

Opening his sack, he jumped upon them.

The sisters quacked and screamed. They flapped and flopped their wings. They flew home and bolted their door.

The next morning, the two Ducks did not go out. They rested at home to quiet their nerves. On the following day they carefully searched for a new and different road. They found one, and it took them safely to the pond.

At times, a change of routine can be most healthful.

KING LION AND THE BEETLE

King Lion looked in the mirror.

"What a beautiful and noble creature I am," he said. "I will go forth to show my devoted subjects that their leader is every inch a king!"

The King put on his robes of state, his large jeweled crown, and all of his gold and silver medals. As he walked down the roads of his kingdom, everyone who saw him bowed to the ground.

"Yes, yes," said King Lion, "I deserve this respect from my people, for truly I *am* every inch a king!"

There was a tiny Beetle standing near the road.

When the King saw him, he cried, "Beetle, I command you to bow low before me!"

"Your Royal Majesty," said the Beetle, "I know that I am small, but if you look at me closely, you will see that I am making a bow."

The King leaned over.

"Beetle," he said, "you are so hard to see down there. I am still not sure that you are bowing."

"Your Majesty," said the Beetle, "please look more closely. I assure you that I am indeed bowing."

The King leaned over a little farther.

Now the robes of state, the large jeweled crown, and all of the gold and silver medals had made King Lion very top-heavy. Suddenly he lost his balance and fell on his head. With a great roar, he rolled into a ditch at the side of the road.

The frightened Beetle scurried away. From head to foot, every inch of King Lion was covered with wet mud.

It is the high and mighty who have the longest distance to fall.

THE LOBSTER AND THE CRAB

On a stormy day, the Crab went strolling along the beach. He was surprised to see the Lobster preparing to set sail in his boat.

"Lobster," said the Crab, "it is foolhardy to venture out on a day like this."

"Perhaps so," said the Lobster, "but I love a squall at sea!"

"I will come with you," said the Crab. "I will not let you face such danger alone."

The Lobster and the Crab began their voyage. Soon they found themselves far from shore. Their boat was tossed and buffeted by the turbulent waters.

"Crab!" shouted the Lobster above the roar of the wind. "For me, the splashing of the salt spray is thrilling! The crashing of every wave takes my breath away!"

"Lobster, I think we are sinking!" cried the Crab.

"Yes, of course, we are sinking," said the Lobster. "This old boat is full of holes. Have courage, my friend. Remember, we are both creatures of the sea."

The little boat capsized and sank.

"Horrors!" cried the Crab.

"Down we go!" shouted the Lobster.

The Crab was shaken and upset. The Lobster took him for a relaxing walk along the ocean floor.

"How brave we are," said the Lobster. "What a wonderful adventure we have had!"

The Crab began to feel somewhat better. Although he usually enjoyed a quieter existence, he had to admit that the day had been pleasantly out of the ordinary.

Even the taking of small risks will add excitement to life.

THE HEN AND THE APPLE TREE

One October day, a Hen looked out her window. She saw an apple tree growing in her backyard.

"Now that is odd," said the Hen. "I am certain that there was no tree standing in that spot yesterday."

"There are some of us that grow fast," said the tree.

The Hen looked at the bottom of the tree.

"I have never seen a tree," she said, "that has ten furry toes."

"There are some of us that do," said the tree. "Hen, come outside and enjoy the cool shade of my leafy branches."

The Hen looked at the top of the tree.

"I have never seen a tree," she said, "that has two long, pointed ears."

"There are some of us that have," said the tree. "Hen, come outside and eat one of my delicious apples."

"Come to think of it," said the Hen, "I have never heard a tree speak from a mouth that is full of sharp teeth."

"There are some of us that can," said the tree. "Hen, come outside and rest your back against the bark of my trunk."

"I have heard," said the Hen, "that some of you trees lose all of your leaves at this time of the year."

"Oh, yes," said the tree, "there are some of us that will." The tree began to quiver and shake. All of its leaves quickly dropped off.

The Hen was not surprised to see a large Wolf in the place where an apple tree had been standing just a moment before. She locked her shutters and slammed her window closed.

The Wolf knew that he had been outsmarted. He stormed away in a hungry rage.

It is always difficult to pose as something that one is not.

THE BABOON'S UMBRELLA

The Baboon was taking his daily walk in the jungle. He met his friend, the Gibbon, on the path.

"My good friend," said the Gibbon, "how strange to find you holding an open umbrella over your head on such a sunshiny day as this."

"Yes," said the Baboon. "I am most annoyed. I cannot close this disagreeable umbrella. It is stuck. I would not think of walking without my umbrella in case it should rain. But, as you see, I am not able to enjoy the sunshine underneath this dark shadow. It is a sad predicament."

"There is a simple solution," said the Gibbon. "You need only to cut some holes in your umbrella. Then the sun will shine on you."

"What a good idea!" cried the Baboon. "I do thank you."

The Baboon ran home. With his scissors, he cut large holes in the top of his umbrella. When the Baboon returned to his walk, the warm sunshine came down through the holes.

"How delightful!" said the Baboon.

However, the sun disappeared behind some clouds. There were a few drops of rain. Then it began to pour. The rain fell through all of the holes in the umbrella. In just a short time, the unhappy Baboon was soaked to the skin.

Advice from friends is like the weather. Some of it is good; some of it is bad.

THE FROGS AT THE RAINBOW'S END

A Frog was swimming in a pond after a rainstorm. He saw a brilliant rainbow stretching across the sky.

"I have heard," said the Frog, "there is a cave filled with gold at the place where the rainbow ends. I will find that cave and be the richest frog in the world!"

The Frog swam to the edge of the pond as fast as he could go. There he met another Frog.

"Where are you rushing to?" asked the second Frog.

"I am rushing to the place where the rainbow ends," said the first Frog.

"There is a rumor," said the second Frog, "that there is a cave filled with gold and diamonds at that place."

"Then come with me," said the first Frog. "We will be the two richest frogs in the world!"

The two Frogs jumped out of the pond and ran through the meadow. There they met another Frog.

"What is the hurry?" asked the third Frog.

"We are running to the place where the rainbow ends," said the two Frogs.

"I have been told," said the third Frog, "there is a cave filled with gold and diamonds and pearls at that place."

"Then come with us," said the two Frogs. "We will be the three richest frogs in the world!"

The three Frogs ran for miles. Finally they came to the rainbow's end. There they saw a dark cave in the side of a hill.

"Gold! Diamonds! Pearls!" cried the Frogs, as they leaped into the cave.

A Snake lived inside. He was hungry and had been thinking about his supper. He swallowed the three Frogs in one quick gulp.

The highest hopes may lead to the greatest disappointments.

THE BEAR AND THE CROW

The Bear was on his way to town. He was dressed in his finest coat and vest. He was wearing his best derby hat and his shiniest shoes.

"How grand I look," said the Bear to himself. "The townsfolk will be impressed. My clothes are at the height of fashion."

"Forgive me for listening," said a Crow, who was sitting on the branch of a tree, "but I must disagree. Your clothes are *not* at the height of fashion. I have just flown in from town. I can tell you exactly how the gentlemen are dressed there."

"Do tell me!" cried the Bear. "I am so eager to wear the most proper attire!"

"This year," said the Crow, "the gentlemen are not wearing hats. They all have frying pans on their heads. They are not wearing coats and vests. They are covering themselves with bed sheets. They are not wearing shoes. They are putting paper bags on their feet."

"Oh, dear," cried the Bear, "my clothes are completely wrong!"

The Bear hurried home. He took off his coat and vest and hat and shoes. He put a frying pan on his head. He wrapped himself in a bed sheet. He stuffed his feet into large paper bags and rushed off toward the town.

When the Bear arrived on Main Street, the people giggled and smirked and pointed their fingers.

"What a ridiculous Bear!" they said.

The embarrassed Bear turned around and ran home. On the way he met the Crow again.

"Crow, you did not tell me the truth!" cried the Bear.

"I told you many things," said the Crow, as he flew out of the tree, "but never once did I tell you that I was telling the truth!"

Even though the Crow was high in the sky, the Bear could still hear the shrill sound of his cackling laughter.

When the need is strong, there are those who will believe anything.

THE CAT AND HIS VISIONS

"What a glorious vision I see in my head!" said the Cat as he went to the riverbank. "I see a large, fat fish on a china plate, resting in an ocean of lemon juice and butter sauce."

He licked his whiskers in anticipation.

The Cat put a worm on a hook and threw his line into the water. He waited for the fish to bite. An hour went by, but nothing happened.

"What a vision I see!" said the Cat. "A fish on a china plate, lying in a lake of lemon juice and butter sauce."

Another hour passed, and nothing happened.

"I see a vision!" said the Cat. "A small fish on a china plate, sprinkled with lemon juice and dribbles of butter sauce."

Many hours later the Cat said, "I can still see a vision. A small, thin fish on a china plate with a little drop of lemon juice and a tiny dab of butter sauce."

After a long time the Cat said sadly, "There is a new vision in my head. I see no fish. I see no lemon juice and not a bit of butter sauce. I see a china plate. It is as empty as my stomach."

The Cat was just about to leave the riverbank when he felt a sudden tug on his line. He pulled a large, fat fish out of the river.

The Cat ran home and fried the fish. He put it on a china plate. He poured a whole ocean of lemon juice and butter sauce all over it.

"What a glorious supper!" said the Cat.

All's well that ends with a good meal.

THE OSTRICH IN LOVE

On Sunday the Ostrich saw a young lady walking in the park. He fell in love with her at once. He followed behind her at a distance, putting his feet in the very places where she had stepped.

On Monday the Ostrich gathered violets as a gift to his beloved. He was too shy to give them to her. He left them at her door and ran away, but there was a great joy in his heart.

On Tuesday the Ostrich composed a song for his beloved. He sang it over and over. He thought it was the most beautiful music he had ever heard.

On Wednesday the Ostrich watched his beloved dining in a restaurant. He forgot to order supper for himself. He was too happy to be hungry.

On Thursday the Ostrich wrote a poem to his beloved. It was the first poem he had ever written, but he did not have the courage to read it to her.

On Friday the Ostrich bought a new suit of clothes. He fluffed his feathers, feeling fine and handsome. He hoped that his beloved might notice.

On Saturday the Ostrich dreamed that he was waltzing with his beloved in a great ballroom. He held her tightly as they whirled around and around to the music. He awoke feeling wonderfully alive.

On Sunday the Ostrich returned to the park. When he saw the young lady walking there, his heart fluttered wildly, but he said to himself, "Alas, it seems that I am much too shy for love. Perhaps another time will come. Yet, surely, this has been a week well spent."

Love can be its own reward.

THE CAMEL DANCES

The Camel had her heart set on becoming a ballet dancer.

"To make every movement a thing of grace and beauty," said the Camel. "That is my one and only desire."

Again and again she practiced her pirouettes, her relevés, and her arabesques. She repeated the five basic positions a hundred times each day. She worked for long months under the hot desert sun. Her feet were blistered, and her body ached with fatigue, but not once did she think of stopping.

At last the Camel said, "Now I am a dancer." She announced a recital and danced before an invited group of camel friends and critics. When her dance was over, she made a deep bow.

There was no applause.

"I must tell you frankly," said a member of the audience, "as a critic and a spokesman for this group, that you are lumpy and humpy. You are baggy and bumpy. You are, like the rest of us, simply a camel. You are *not* and never will be a ballet dancer!"

Chuckling and laughing, the audience moved away across the sand.

"How very wrong they are!" said the Camel. "I have worked hard. There can be no doubt that I am a splendid dancer. I will dance and dance just for myself."

That is what she did. It gave her many years of pleasure.

Satisfaction will come to those who please themselves.

THE POOR OLD DOG

There was an old Dog who was very poor. The only coat he had to wear was mostly holes held together by ragged threads. He could feel the pebbles on the pavement through the thin soles of his tattered shoes. He slept in the park because he had no home.

The Dog spent most of his time searching in garbage cans. He found bits of string and buttons. These he sold for pennies to passersby.

The Dog always walked with his nose close to the curb, looking for things to sell. That is how he came to find the gold ring that was lying in the gutter.

"My luck has changed," cried the Dog, "for I am sure that this is a magic ring!"

The Dog rubbed the ring and said, "I wish for a new coat. I wish for new shoes. I wish for a house to live in. I wish these wishes would come true right now!"

But nothing happened. The Dog felt the wind through the holes in his coat. He felt the pebbles under his thin shoes. That night he slept on his usual bench in the park.

Several days later, the Dog saw a note on a lamppost. The note said "Lost: gold ring. Large reward. Mr. Terrier. Ten Wealthy Lane."

The old Dog hurried to Wealthy Lane. Mr. Terrier was overjoyed to have his ring returned. He thanked the Dog profusely and gave him a bulging purse that was full of coins.

The Dog bought a warm fur coat. He bought a pair of good shoes with thick soles.

There was a large amount of money left over. The Dog used the rest of it as a down payment on a cozy little house. He moved right in and never had to sleep in the park again.

Wishes, on their way to coming true, will not be rushed.

25

MADAME RHINOCEROS AND HER DRESS

Madame Rhinoceros saw a dress in the window of a shop. It was covered with polka dots and flowers. It was adorned with ribbons and lace. She admired it for a moment and then entered the shop.

"That dress in the window," said Madame Rhinoceros to a salesperson, "I would like to try it on."

Madame Rhinoceros put on the dress. She looked at herself in the mirror. "I do not think this dress is at all attractive on me," she said.

"But Madame," said the salesperson, "you are completely wrong. This dress makes you look glamorous and alluring."

"If only I were sure," said Madame Rhinoceros.

"Ah, Madame," said the salesperson, "everyone who sees you wearing this dress will be filled with admiration and envy."

"Do you really think so?" asked Madame Rhinoceros, turning around and around in front of the mirror.

"Absolutely," said the salesperson. "You have my word."

"Very well," said Madame Rhinoceros, "I will buy the dress, and I will wear it now."

Madame Rhinoceros left the shop. As she walked up the avenue, she saw that people were smiling and laughing at her.

"Admiration," thought Madame Rhinoceros.

She saw some people who were shaking their heads and frowning.

"Envy," thought Madame Rhinoceros.

She continued up the avenue. Everyone who saw her stopped and stared. Madame Rhinoceros felt more glamorous and alluring with every step.

Nothing is harder to resist than a bit of flattery.

THE BAD KANGAROO

There was a small Kangaroo who was bad in school. He put thumb-tacks on the teacher's chair. He threw spitballs across the classroom. He set off firecrackers in the lavatory and spread glue on the doorknobs.

"Your behavior is impossible!" said the school principal. "I am going to see your parents. I will tell them what a problem you are!"

The principal went to visit Mr. and Mrs. Kangaroo. He sat down in a living-room chair.

"Ouch!" cried the principal. "There is a thumbtack in this chair!"

"Yes, I know," said Mr. Kangaroo. "I enjoy putting thumbtacks in chairs."

A spitball hit the principal on his nose.

"Forgive me," said Mrs. Kangaroo, "but I can never resist throwing those things."

There was a loud booming sound from the bathroom.

"Keep calm," said Mr. Kangaroo to the principal. "The firecrackers that we keep in the medicine chest have just exploded. We love the noise."

The principal rushed for the front door. In an instant he was stuck to the doorknob.

"Pull hard," said Mrs. Kangaroo. "There are little globs of glue on all of our doorknobs."

The principal pulled himself free. He dashed out of the house and ran off down the street.

"Such a nice person," said Mr. Kangaroo. "I wonder why he left so quickly."

"No doubt he had another appointment," said Mrs. Kangaroo. "Never mind, supper is ready."

Mr. and Mrs. Kangaroo and their son enjoyed their evening meal. After the dessert, they all threw spitballs at each other across the dining-room table.

A child's conduct will reflect the ways of his parents.

THE PIG AT THE CANDY STORE

All night long, the sleeping Pig dreamed of candy. He sprouted wings of spun sugar. He flew up through marshmallow clouds to a glowing marzipan moon. The stars that twinkled in the sky were chocolate kisses wrapped in shiny foil.

The Pig woke up with his mouth watering.

"Candy!" he cried. "I must have some this minute!"

The Pig ran to the candy dish. It was empty. The box of chocolate creams in the cupboard contained nothing but paper wrappers.

"I will go to the candy store," said the Pig, as he put on his clothes and rushed out of his house.

"On second thought," said the Pig, "I must remember that candy is bad for me. It makes me fatter than I already am. It gives me gas and heartburn."

Then the Pig remembered his sweet dreams. He decided that since he was halfway to the candy store, he might as well finish the journey.

"Just a few peppermints will not hurt me," he said.

As the Pig came near the store, his mouth began to water again. "Maybe I will buy a small bag of gumdrops as well," he said.

But the candy store was closed. A sign on the door said "On Vacation."

The Pig went back home.

"What wonderful willpower I have!" he cried happily. "I did not eat a single piece of candy!"

That night the Pig had a vegetable salad for supper. He drank a glass of cold, fresh milk. He felt thin and had neither gas nor heartburn.

A locked door is very likely to discourage temptation.

31

THE ELEPHANT AND HIS SON

The Elephant and his son were spending an evening at home. Elephant Son was singing a song.

"You must be silent," said Father Elephant. "Your papa is trying to read his newspaper. Papa cannot listen to a song while he is reading his newspaper."

"Why not?" asked Elephant Son.

"Because Papa can think about only one thing at a time, that is why," said Father Elephant.

Elephant Son stopped singing. He sat quietly. Father Elephant lit a cigar and went on reading.

After a while, Elephant Son asked, "Papa, can you still think about only one thing at a time?"

"Yes, my boy," said Father Elephant, "that is correct."

"Well then," said Elephant Son, "you might stop thinking about your newspaper and begin to think about the slipper that is on your left foot."

"But my boy," said Father Elephant, "Papa's newspaper is far more important and interesting and informative than the slipper that is on his left foot."

"That may be true," said Elephant Son, "but while your newspaper is not on fire from the ashes of your cigar, the slipper that is on your left foot certainly is!"

Father Elephant ran to put his foot in a bucket of water. Softly, Elephant Son began to sing again.

Knowledge will not always take the place of simple observation.

THE PELICAN AND THE CRANE

The Crane invited the Pelican to tea.

"So nice of you to ask me to come," said the Pelican to the Crane. "No one invites me anywhere."

"Entirely my pleasure," said the Crane to the Pelican, passing him the sugar bowl. "Do you take sugar in your tea?"

"Yes, thank you," said the Pelican. He dumped half the sugar into his cup, while spilling the other half on the floor.

"I seem to have no friends at all," said the Pelican.

"Do you take milk in your tea?" asked the Crane.

"Yes, thank you," said the Pelican. He poured some of the milk into his cup, but most of it made a puddle on the table.

"I wait and wait," said the Pelican. "Nobody ever calls me."

"Will you have a cookie?" asked the Crane.

"Yes, thank you," said the Pelican. He took a large pile of cookies and stuffed them into his mouth. His shirtfront was covered with crumbs.

"I hope you will invite me again," said the Pelican.

"Perhaps," said the Crane, "but I am so very busy these days."

"Good-bye until the next time," said the Pelican. He swallowed many more cookies. He wiped his mouth with the tablecloth and left.

After the Pelican had gone, the Crane shook his head and sighed. He called for his maid to clean up the mess.

When one is a social failure, the reasons are as clear as day.

THE YOUNG ROOSTER

A young Rooster was summoned to his Father's bedside. "Son, my time has come to an end," said the aged bird. "Now it is your turn to crow up the morning sun each day."

The young Rooster watched sadly as his Father's life slipped away.

Early the next morning, the young Rooster flew up to the roof of the barn. He stood there, facing the east.

"I have never done this before," said the Rooster. "I must try my best." He lifted his head and crowed. A weak and scratchy croak was the only sound he was able to make.

The sun did not come up. Clouds covered the sky, and a damp drizzle fell all day. All of the animals of the farm came to the Rooster.

"This is a disaster!" cried a Pig.

"We need our sunshine!" shouted a Sheep.

"Rooster, you must crow much louder," said a Bull. "The sun is ninety-three million miles away. How do you expect it to hear you?"

Very early the next morning, the young Rooster flew up to the roof of the barn again. He took a deep breath, he threw back his head and CROWED. It was the loudest crow that was ever crowed since the beginning of roosters.

The animals on the farm were awakened from their sleep with a start.

"What a noise!" cried the Pig.

"My ears hurt!" shouted the Sheep.

"My head is splitting!" said the Bull.

"I am sorry," said the Rooster, "but I was only doing my job."

He said this with a great deal of pride, for he saw, far to the east, the tip of the morning sun coming up over the trees.

A first failure may prepare the way for later success.

THE HIPPOPOTAMUS AT DINNER

The Hippopotamus went into a restaurant. He sat at his favorite table. "Waiter!" called the Hippopotamus. "I will have the bean soup, the Brussels sprouts, and the mashed potatoes. Please hurry, I am enormously hungry tonight!"

In a short while, the waiter returned with the order. The Hippopotamus glared down at his plate.

"Waiter," he said, "do you call this a meal? These portions are much too small. They would not satisfy a bird. I want a *bathtub* of bean soup, a *bucket* of Brussels sprouts, and a *mountain* of mashed potatoes. I tell you I have an APPETITE!"

The waiter went back into the kitchen. He returned carrying enough bean soup to fill a bathtub, enough Brussels sprouts to fill a bucket, and a mountain of mashed potatoes. In no time, the Hippopotamus had eaten every last morsel.

"Delicious!" said the Hippopotamus, as he dabbed his mouth with a napkin and prepared to leave.

To his surprise, he could not move. His stomach, which had grown considerably larger, was caught between the table and the chair. He pulled and tugged, but it was no use. He could not budge.

The hour grew late. The other customers in the restaurant finished their dinners and left. The cooks took off their aprons and put away their pots. The waiters cleared the dishes and turned out the lights. They all went home.

The Hippopotamus remained there, sitting forlornly at the table.

"Perhaps I should not have eaten quite so many Brussels sprouts," he said, as he gazed into the gloom of the darkened restaurant. Occasionally, he burped.

Too much of anything often leaves one with a feeling of regret.

THE MOUSE AT THE SEASHORE

A Mouse told his mother and father that he was going on a trip to the seashore.

"We are very alarmed!" they cried. "The world is full of terrors. You must not go!"

"I have made my decision," said the Mouse firmly. "I have never seen the ocean, and it is high time that I did. Nothing can make me change my mind."

"Then we cannot stop you," said Mother and Father Mouse, "but do be careful!"

The next day, in the first light of dawn, the Mouse began his journey. Even before the morning had ended, the Mouse came to know trouble and fear.

A Cat jumped out from behind a tree.

"I will eat you for lunch," he said.

It was a narrow escape for the Mouse. He ran for his life, but he left a part of his tail in the mouth of the Cat.

By afternoon the Mouse had been attacked by birds and dogs. He had lost his way several times. He was bruised and bloodied. He was tired and frightened.

At evening the Mouse slowly climbed the last hill and saw the seashore spreading out before him. He watched the waves rolling onto the beach, one after another. All the colors of the sunset filled the sky.

"How beautiful!" cried the Mouse. "I wish that Mother and Father were here to see this with me."

The moon and the stars began to appear over the ocean. The Mouse sat silently on the top of the hill. He was overwhelmed by a feeling of deep peace and contentment.

All the miles of a hard road are worth a moment of true happiness.

Typography design by Kohar Alexanian
Set in 12/16 Linotype Electra,
with display in foundry Caslon Open and Caslon No. 540
Composed by Boro Typographers, Inc.
Color Separations by Offset Separations Corp.
Lithography by Federated Lithographers-Printers, Inc.
Bound by Publishers Book Bindery, Inc.
Printed on 80 lb. Patina Matte
Harper & Row, Publishers, Inc.